First published in hardback in Great Britain
by HarperCollins Children's Books in 2005
First published in paperback in 2006

1 3 5 7 9 10 8 6 4 2

ISBN-13: 978-0-00-722593-4
ISBN-10: 0-00-722593-8

HarperCollins Children's Books is a division of HarperCollins Publishers Ltd.

Visit our website at: www.harpercollinschildrensbooks.co.uk

Printed in China

Melrose and Croc

TOGETHER AT CHRISTMAS

by Emma Chichester Clark

HarperCollins *Children's Books*

One day, before Christmas, a small green crocodile walked down a busy street, carrying a suitcase. Not far away, a yellow dog called Melrose was opening his front door.

Little Green Croc had come to the city to see
Father Christmas at the big department store.

He was so excited. He looked at the piece of paper again. It said:

"Come and meet
FATHER CHRISTMAS
at Harridges!
Make your dreams
come true!"

"Tomorrow,"
thought Croc,
"will be wonderful."

Melrose had also just arrived in town. He was decorating his new apartment. "I wish I had somebody to do this with," he said to himself. "I wish someone else could see them."

He looked at the box of Christmas tree decorations.

"I may as well put these away again," he thought.

"There's no point in having a tree, just for me."

That night, as Melrose gazed at the view, he sighed,
"It's Christmas; I should be happy, but I feel sad."

Little Green Croc looked out at the great
dark sea. He was too excited even to sleep.

In the morning, Croc arrived at Harridges.

"Can you tell me the way to Father Christmas?" he asked.

"Oh, I'm afraid you've missed him," said the manager.

"He was here last week. He's busy now. It *is* Christmas Eve."

Croc felt like crying, but he didn't want people to see.

"I'm hopeless," thought Croc. "I've got everything wrong… and now I'm soaked!" Little Green Croc burst into tears. It didn't matter anymore.

Melrose hadn't seen Croc or the puddle. He was
still finding his way around town. "I wish I could
find a way to cheer up," he thought.

"And I wish I could find a friend," he sighed.

A lady was giving away surprise presents.

"For you to share," she smiled.

"Thank you," said Melrose, sadly.

Croc found a place to shelter from the snow.
"How foolish I was to come," he thought. A tear
dropped on to his suitcase. Then suddenly he
heard music, lovely music. It rang through the
air and he followed it...

Little Green Croc forgot everything.

He whirled and twirled. He glided and slid.

Melrose was there, whirling too. He flew, faster
than light. He felt lighter than air.

"If only I could skate forever!" thought Melrose. "If only I could just skate forever…" thought Croc. They swooped and looped. They zig-zagged left and right… faster and faster… until…

CRASH!

"OW!" cried Melrose.
"OH!" cried Croc.

"I'm so sorry!" gasped Croc.

"No, *I'm* sorry!" said Melrose. "Come on, let's go
and have some tea."

They sat and told each other everything.

"…and now Christmas is ruined," Croc finished.

Then Melrose had a brilliant idea.

"Come and spend Christmas with me!" he cried.

"We'll get a tree, and Father Christmas will come!"

Croc wiped the last tear off his nose.

"I'd love to do that," he said.

While Melrose cooked dinner, Little Green Croc
decorated the tree.

"Look!" cried Melrose, "I told you he'd come!
There he is!"

The next day was Christmas Day.

"All my dreams are coming true!" said Croc.

"Mine too," said Melrose. "All I wanted was a friend and I found you!"

"And I found *you*! Happy Christmas," smiled Croc.

Have you read all the stories about Melrose and Croc?

Melrose and Croc
FIND A SMILE

ISBN: 0-00-718241-4

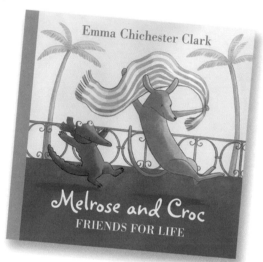

Melrose and Croc
FRIENDS FOR LIFE

ISBN: 0-00-718242-2

All £5.99

Melrose and Croc
GO TO TOWN

ISBN: 0-00-718243-0
Publishing July 2007

Melrose and Croc
BESIDE THE SEA

ISBN: 0-00-718244-9
Publishing April 2007